When the CROCODILES Came to Town

For Neli, Mia and Daniel

ORCHARD BOOKS

First published in Great Britain in 2019
by The Watts Publishing Group

10 9 8 7 6 5 4 3 2 1

Text and illustrations © Magda Brol, 2019

A CIP catalogue record for this book is
available from the British Library.

HB ISBN 978 1 40835 087 4
PB ISBN 978 1 40835 088 1

Printed and bound in China

Orchard Books
An imprint of Hachette Children's Group
Part of The Watts Publishing Group Limited
Carmelite House 50 Victoria Embankment
London EC4Y 0DZ

An Hachette UK Company
www.hachette.co.uk

www.hachettechildrens.co.uk

FSC
MIX
Paper from
responsible sources
www.fsc.org FSC® C104740

When the CROCODILES Came to Town

DULLSVILLE

Magda Brol

ORCHARD

WELCOME TO DULLSVILLE

WINNER OF THE 1952 GOLDEN DONKEY AWARD FOR
WORLD'S MOST BORING TOWN

No one knew why
the crocodiles
came to our town.

It was clear from the very beginning ...

They didn't look like us.

... they didn't fit in.

Or behave like us.

They did very odd things...

... at very
odd times.

They didn't seem to understand the rules:

THE DULLSVILLE RULES

1. KEEP IT TIDY
2. KEEP IT QUIET
3. KEEP IT PLAIN
4. KEEP OFF THE GOLDEN DONKEY

Mayor Moody

This annoyed everyone, especially the mayor. "Get off my donkey!" he barked.

Then, market day came round ...

... and the crocs got it wrong AGAIN.

"Ice cream treats for everyone!" they shouted. "Try our delicious ice cream ... and strawberry sauce!"

But the people of my town did NOT like ice cream. They didn't like anything messy or fun. Enough was enough, they decided. These crocs did not belong ...

The message was LOUD and CLEAR.

But, that night,
as the crocs were
packing to leave...

... someone else
was arriving.

Glen and Freda Grabbit were the
**NAUGHTIEST THIEVES
IN THE LAND.**

As they crept through

our sleeping town ...

... they stole from every house.

But what
they REALLY
wanted was ...

BUMP! CLATTER! CRASH!
... they didn't notice two
clumsy crocs, making
their way out of town!

WELL ...

... and SNEAKY.
The chase went on all night.

... those thieves were FAST.

But the crocs had a secret weapon: SUPER STICKY ICE CREAM SAUCE!

They raced through the streets with a

RUMBLE, BUMP, SQUELCH, until ...

Hurrah!

That's me

Glen and Freda Grabbit met a
VERY STICKY END.

"Hurrah! Hurrah for the crocs!"
I yelled. "Oh, please, Mr Mayor...

"LET THE CROCS STAY!"

The mayor took a very deep breath.

"Um...   Er...   Ahem...

"I'm sorry, Crocs. We got you all wrong.
You belong in our town.
YOU CAN STAY –
and so can your ice cream."

And that was that.

Glen and Freda Grabbit
were never seen again.

And the crocs?

We never found out
where they came from.

We never knew why they
had chosen our town.

But we welcomed them ...

WELCOME TO
CROCS
DULLSVILLE

... EXACTLY AS
THEY WERE.